homodeus

An Introduction to the Ineffable

A Selection of Poems By Joe

JOSEPH F. EDWARDS

Printed Worldwide
First Printing 2025
First Edition 2025

10 9 8 7 6 5 4 3 2 1
ISBN 978-0-9836530-3-5

Published by Cara Press

Interior Book Design by Walt's Book Design
www.waltsbookdesign.com

Contact: permissions@carapress.com

homodeus

homodeus

homo: man
deus: God

We all have poetry in us, and we all have those poetic moments which push us ever so slightly closer to that which cannot be bounded by the human word. Our poetry leads us toward the ineffable.

CONTENTS

FOREWORD

I used to be a young poet. Now I am an old poet. I wrote The Opposite Shore no later than 1963. That was sixty-one years ago. I still read it. I still read all of my poetry because it gives me an experience like nothing else can. Poetry is layered like no other form of literature, and these layers interact with each other and sometimes exchange places within the hierarchy of layers, and we are transported. This is an experience that is just as real as any that a thinker can summon through philosophical analysis, and it is just flat out more fun getting there through poetry.

Sometimes a poem doesn't make sense. It just works. I don't know what else to say about that. You'll probably hit a couple of those in this selection. And honestly, they may not work on you the way they work on me. But I hope they do.

I have used some of these poems as passages in Homo, which is included in my novel Sanctified, and since I see it as a long poem itself that is a major part of my work, I include it in this selection. Yes, you can reuse poems. Over and over. They are linguistic, spiritual, experiential building blocks. Nobody can tell you or me what we can do with them.

Joe

CRISTOLOGO

A train whose name was Yesterday
Came thundering down that track.
You know the one.
That same track on which Tomorrow
thundered in....
From east and west
A hundred thousand tons of steel
Came screaming,
Screaming down that track,
And crashed....
The track is gone,
The steel is gone,
The thing is done.
But if you will come along with me,
I will show you where it happened:
I was there,
Sitting on a bench,
In a little station,
In a village whose name was Now,
Waiting to catch my train.

STARDUST

When the stardust settles
and the glitter eases
and does not matter,
and when the sharp has dulled
and the high notes ring less shrill and strident,
and the numbers matter less,
or matter not at all,
and when tomorrow teases
and does not threaten,
and yesterday recedes
and today is here,
and we have each said to the other
Well done,
I look at you one last time,
one last time,
before they close it.

ODE TO THE RULE

They came to measure me,
four of'em plus the main guy,
who's not as big as they are.
They take out this thing they call a rule,
made of high quality durable hardwood, they explain,
and unfold it and hold it up against me,
and make sure they've got it right at one end,
which they call an extremity,
and they say I've got an imaginary perpendicular there,
which you can't see,
which is why they call it imaginary,
I suppose,
but one guy puts a stick on top of my head just to make sure,
and he doesn't hit me with it.

They say not to worry about it —
it's just imaginary without the stick,
and the stick helps them see the perpendicular you can't see,
and I say how do you know the stick's really perpendicular
if you don't have a tool to check that,
and they say it's close enough,
and they say I'm this long and they point.

"That's you, right there,"
and they show me me on the unfolded rule,
and I'm just speechless because I can't see me right there,
where they are pointing.
All I see are numbers and various little lines.
But I guess if they say that's me, that's me.
Who am I to say?

And then they leave, starting with the little guy,
who just walks out,
and doesn't even look back at me.
But then the big guys walk out backwards,
all four of'em, one by one,
and they each look right at me,
the whole time they are backing out.
Weird…

And then the next time they measure me,
not too long after the first time, maybe a few weeks,
or it could have been a few months —
I'm pretty sure it was not as long as a year,
same four plus the main guy,
presumably with the same high quality durable hardwood
rule
(it certainly looks like the same one),
which they unfold,
and place precisely on my imaginary perpendicular,

at the same part of me they called an extremity last time,
which I believe was the top of my head,
if I recall correctly,
they say I'm a little short,
I've shrunk a little,
and they say to each other…
"He's a little short; he's shrunk a little,
probably due to some spinal compression," they say,
"probably has a little osteoporosis;
we'll monitor this,"
and they fold up the unfolded rule, that has brass joints.
Or at least the main dude folds up the unfolded rule,
that has brass joints,
and he writes all this down in a little book,
which I take to be the monitor.

So I'm both long and short?
Well that's crazy, but I didn't say anything.
If you open your mouth around here they think you're crazy.

Over the last few days,
or frankly it could be the last few weeks,
I've really been thinking about this,
and I'm pretty sure I've got it figured out,
and just for you who don't live here,
and who have at least some interest in what I am trying to

explain to you,
if you would just listen,

here's the long and the short of it:
or I should say here's the long and the short of me, not it:

There's some guy out there,
who can tell guys much bigger than him what to do,
sort of a Leader,
out there with a Rule,
made of high quality durable hardwood,
with brass joints no less,
(I saw'em — the brass joints — when they were unfolding
the rule,
and placing it against my imaginary perpendicular,
and I know brass when I see it),
some dude going around out there with four big guys,
and I mean BIG,
and all wearing the same kind of clothes, and the same color,
(except there was something different about the little guy,
but I can't quite put my finger on it),
coming into people's rooms
measuring for longs and shorts.
Apparently the Leader needs to know who's long and who's
short,
or maybe it's for even a BIGGER Leader above him.
But the way I see it, one way or the other it's for a Leader,

whether he's big or little,
or both.

I'll be honest with you: If I see'em comin' down the hall,
or comin' out of somebody else's room,
I'm going to scoot right back to my room,
so I'll be there,
in case they need to measure me again.

I kinda like that rule.
I love those brass joints,
and the way it stretches out and gets longer
when the little guy unfolds it (he's actually really nice,
even though he didn't look at me when he left).
And I'm pretty sure I still have my imaginary perpendicular
for it,
but if not, I'm sure they'll have one they can use.
I just don't think it's my responsibility to store up imaginary
perpendiculars,
especially for somebody else to use, for who knows what.
I mean, somebody could do some serious damage with that
kind of stuff,
especially when you can't even see'em.
But I'm not going to worry about that.
I've got enough to worry about.

What is a Poem?

A poem is a struggle,
to say the unsayable,
a call to divinity,
to pray the unprayable.

Oops. Forgive me; I fell into rhyme.
The modern technique is to seek the sublime
by leading the reader with cadence and time,
and writing in prose and hoping to score
the same thing today as we did before.
Slap my face!
Sorry, I'll switch….
(Mais où sont les neiges d'antan?)

A poem is puppy breath,
perhaps even the pup,
but certainly the breath.
It signals the ineffable,
but always fails:
the ineffable is still ineffable,
and always will be,
notwithstanding the poem.
(I've been poeming for over sixty years; take my word for it).
It helps you almost see what cannot be seen,

almost hear what cannot be heard.
Almost.

A poem is a door knob….
There. See?

(Might be a decent middle for a haiku,
except I guarantee you some literary troublemaker
will say the word poem only has one syllable: like pome,
and the middle of a haiku needs seven,
as everyone on the planet knows.
It just never ends.).

A poem is a thing, a thing that derails you,
and makes you glad you were thrown off the track.

If you don't believe a poem is a thing, read my essay
The Ontology of a Poem
which I may write someday.
(I'm also a philosopher
but poetry's more fun;
the philosopher just sits,
while the poet's on a run!)
Oh man, my cheek's starting to sting….

Poets have a tiny audience, a great man once told me,
which is fine by me.

Some poets have an audience of one, I responded.
(If you are reading this,
I at least have an audience of two:
an audience of me,
and an audience of you).
Oops. Careful. Sorry. Ouch!
I really need to work on that….

I am a poet.
I've been poeming for over sixty years.
To be honest,
I really don't know what a poem is.

But here's a haiku:

What is a poem?
Puppy breath is a poem.
I want a puppy.

Count'em. 5, 7, 5

HOMODEUS

Prolegomena to Any Future Metaphysics
(With Apologies to Immanuel Kant)

deus
homo
homodeus
deus

A Poem in Spite of Me

I don't have time to write poems today;
I don't even have time to pray.
Oops.
Pardon the redundancy.

The Earth

One ocean,
The rest, land.

Hairy, fuzzy, footy, feathery, scaly
endoskeletal and exoskeletal life on the land;

Wiggly, slimy, slippery, scaly, swimmy
endoskeletal and exoskeletal life in the seas;

some in both.

Me?
Hairy, handy, fuzzy, footy,
most of the time;

and only sometimes
wiggly, slimy, slippery, scaly, swimmy;

But always endoskeletal.

Stardust 2

When the stardust settles
and the glitter dims
and does not matter,
and when the sharp has dulled
and the high notes ring less shrill and strident,
and the numbers matter less,
or matter not at all,
and when tomorrow teases
and does not threaten,
and yesterday recedes
and today is here,
and our time has come,
our white hair flowing in the gentle breeze,
we stroll hand in hand,
into the sunset.

Honeybees of Edinburgh

There's a honey man in Scotland,
on that seventh mountain over,
who weekly goes to Edinburgh
with honey made from clover.

He leaves his bees on the mountainside
to work while he's away,
and hawks their honey in Edinburgh
while they stay home and play.

Watch out little man on the mountain,
you'll soon run out of honey.
You think your bees are working
while you chase after money.

But play they will, those bees you keep,
no matter where you roam;
for honey bees near Edinburgh,
will swarm when you're not home.

THE RESOLUTION

The hunter crouched in the glade, in the tall grass,
And slowly, silently, took one long arrow from his pouch,
And nocked it; he must not let this moment pass,
Without its long awaited, long sought resolution.
The hunted paused, in the shade, by the tall grass,
And rested, kneeling, full aware that his ablution,
In the temple, had resolved nothing alas,
For the one who would have his soul, who crouched in the
glade.
The hunter aimed his arrow, from the tall grass,
And drew it; and every fiber in him tensed, replayed
The passions of a thousand pains that would never pass,
And then released. Watching, the hunter slowly rose from
his crouch.

High, High Fly the Yearning Spirits

High, high fly the yearning spirits;
High fly the seekers;
High fly the comers and the goers,
And the gazers at the comers and the goers,
And the gazers at these;
And the greeters and the talkers -
Ah, the greeters and the talkers -
How high they fly…

Then Slowly Out of the Night They Came

Then slowly out of the night they came.
Slowly, out of the bedded leaves,
from deep in the caves,
stretching and gazing about they came,
moving away from the dens,
and the night,
and the night mind,
and out onto the pebbly slopes,
leading down below,
where the dew-tender grains of the wild-grass patch awaited
them.

And the poet was the one
who watched the ones
who watched the ones
who gathered grain in the wild-grass patch.

I Know You Homo

I know you, Homo.
I've looked out across you,
And seen the whole of you,
And seen your comings and your goings,
Homo;
And I've seen you recline as one across whole lands,
And I've seen you rise all with the dawn,
And take up your tools and your weapons,
And set out upon your roads and your byways,
And into the forests,
And assert yourself.
And your groupings of habitations have amazed me, Homo.
Domus!
Civitatem! How can I speak of them?
How can I tell of the application of your paws
To the earth and the stone and the wood,
And the mixing of your mortar,
And the shaping of your spikes,
And then with them the making of your hut,
And then the placing of another and another
Till there are many, together?
You congregate, Homo!
I have long sought to view you from a metaspecial
perspective,

And yet I cannot do it;
I cannot do it completely, Homo,
For your utterances make sense to me,
And your motions are my motions:
There have been times when I would have
Locked my paw around a club,
And a stout one, too!
And set out meanly upon the trail
Toward your agglomeration
To injure and to kill:
I know you Homo.

I Am The Storyteller's Poet

I am the storyteller's poet,
Admirer of threads and of
threads of threads,
And willing talker thereabout.
I seek all their connections.
I am that percipient essence before which
there is the ceaseless query.
Perhaps it could even be said of me
that I am the query.
(It is true that from time to time
I succumb to the machinations of man;
But in the end I am true to you,
My Song,
For in the end it is the poet who sings.)

My Mare I Mount

My mare I mount, and she gathers.
She gathers and she holds.
(No tears my lady – who can at once
weep and sing?)
She gathers, till we can no more.
She holds, till we can no more.
Princess?
And then together
We fly!

WE KNOW NOT WHY

We know not why the roles of yesterday
were played,
Nor why tomorrow's greatest dreams
are never lived.
We know not yet why blood was spilled
and children cried,
(All the children God has made
have cried)
Nor why tomorrow blood and tears
will flow again.
But this we know:
Now this we know:
In a little room, in a little house,
we make love today.

Sound the Cadence!

Sound the cadence!
Stomp, Stomp,
Here or there a pleasure,
On beyond a woe.
Stomp, Stomp,
On down through the halls of time
We make our way.

A Night Wanderer You Have Caused Me To Be

A night wanderer you have caused me to be,

A star gazer uncertain,

Till you settle about me

And speak truth to me.

Engage me!

Do not hesitate to trust me with your

cherished knowledge.

Teach me your secrets –

I'll harbor them and use them,

and I'll pass them on to those,

And those only,

Who should have them.

GONE

Gone, my Love, are the high winds and the
soaring eagles.
Grim is the night.
Dim are the night beings and the night mind;
Gone is the light.

THE STORY OF SAMMY DEVEAU

This is the story of Sammy Deveau,
Who lived his life as a wandering child.
He ate and played and appeared to grow,
But poor young Sammy was always reviled.

Few were his talents in worldly affairs,
And nothing great did Sammy pretend.
The town viewed Sammy as one of its tares,
A wandering waif on whom none could depend.

The town kept growing with Sammy in tow,
Until the elders and the rich convened:
"We must do something with Sammy Deveau,
Help him mature or we'll all be demeaned!"
"Look at his clothes and his beard and his tears!
He must not have groomed in more than a week!"
And so these great men, to allay their fears,
Set something aside for Sammy the freak.

They gave him shoes and a shave and some bread,
They bought him a suit and a shirt and tie.

Then they all looked close and nodded and said,
"Sammy, we're done, now you give it a try!"

So Sammy went out and roamed about town,
And did what he could to hide all his fears;
But now our Sammy has gone way, way down;
Now our Sammy is awash in his tears.

Yes, now our Sammy has gone way, way down,
He's a wandering soul alone in town:
A dangerous wave on a placid sea;
He's coming for you; he's coming for me.

The Opposite Shore

From among those beings in the dim
past he had wandered, and had gone on.
Why? He had asked, and had gone on,
till he came to the brink of the deep, and
looked.
It is too late, he said.
And the chasm returned with the reply,
Why?
He died! He cried.
Said the chasm, Who?
Me!
You?
Yes, he muttered, and gazed,
From the brink of the deep,
To the opposite shore.
Said the chasm, Where?
There, he said, and pointed from the
brink to the opposite shore.
Then why are you here?
Here?
I don't know, he said, and gazed,
from the brink of the deep,
to the opposite shore.

THIS THING

It's there in the storyteller's soul,
And in the marble cornerstone
of homo's domicile,
This thing that moves on
through us all,
And does not stop when
each we do,
But moves on,
Becoming more with
each birth,
And yet even more with
each demise,
Transversing generations and
constituting them each,
Expressing them all,
And being expressed by them,
This thing.

God All

God All.
God the tree.
God the bird. God grass.
God fences and pastures.
God cows, horses, mules, and pigs.
God leaves, water, and stone.
God the highs, God the hassles, God the smooth sailing.
God the illusions of man,
God you, God me,
God All.

Go

Go into the night!
Count every star in the heavens.
Go roam the valleys,
And climb the mountains,
And sail the oceans:
Then come to me and let me gently
whisper in your ear;
I'll say to you, In all time,
You will not see what I have perceived
in one timeless flash.

FROM MY SOUL WILL I SING

I've stood at the foot of the mountain
and looked up.
I've soared to the peak
and looked down.
I've stood inside
and looked out,
I've stood outside
and looked in.

So know you this:
From my soul will I sing as much as from my mind.
If thinker you would have me
always be,
You will go wanting,
For poet I am,
I am.

HAIKU

Haiku is special. It has tight parameters that force the poet to think and explore. This usually results in a satisfying poem, but occasionally it produces a profound thought bomb that takes poet and reader to another place. It is a wonderful way to seek and then express truth. It reaches for the ineffable. Sometimes, sometimes, it almost succeeds.

Bright White Clouds

~ 37 ~

Bright white clouds roll in,
against a vast azure sky.
Then the dark clouds come.

SHE SUCKLES HER PUP

She suckles her pup.
She sighs and raises her head,
and licks her blind pup.

Rain On My Garden

~ 39 ~

Rain on my garden,
wets the freshly sprouted plants,
including the weeds.

She Planted An Elm

She planted an elm.
It grew and shaded my yard.
Then she chopped it down.

Brooks Into Rivers

~ 41 ~

Brooks into rivers.
Then rivers into oceans,
then oceans to rain.

We Swim In The Rain

Rain falls and makes brooks;
and brooks flow into rivers.
We swim in the rain.

OUR CRUTCH

~ 43 ~

Haiku is our crutch.
We meditate with Haiku,
and the poems flow.

How Wolves Eat Grass

The grass grows all night.
Our sheep eat the grass all day.
Then wolves eat some sheep.

How to Lessen the Amount of Grass

The grass grows all night.

Our sheep eat the grass all day.

Now we kill some wolves.

HOW WE EAT GRASS

The grass grows all night.
Our sheep eat the grass all day.
Now we eat some sheep.

CLIMB THAT MOUNTAIN

~ 47 ~

Go climb that mountain,
that mountain inside of you.
Then come home to me.

WAIT

Fall is now complete;
But winter storms are blowing.
This must wait til spring.

Rain Falls

~ 49 ~

Rain falls on the earth.
The grass grows and feeds the sheep.
Then it rains again.

Rain Falls II

Rain falls on the earth.
The grass grows and feeds the sheep.
Shepherds guard their flocks.

Lord God Send Us Rain

(Two Ancient Prayers)

Lord God send us rain!

Rain falls, pastures grow, sheep eat.

Lord God save your flock!

Mixed

When The Pigs Begin To Prance

When the ducks begin to sing,
and when the pigs begin to prance,
and when the surgeons start to quack,
and when the lawyers and the judges
start to waddle in their fat,
and when the bishops beg for cash,
and when the preachers look away,
and when the teachers teach their lies,
and when the merchants overcharge,
and then belch,
that's when the masses start to rise,
and sing of life beyond the track,
a song of getting something back,
whatever they can get,
before whatever can't be got.

From here we hear the rumble,
of the song beyond the track.
And so from here we scramble,
on this side,
like the pilots of the killer jets,
to quickly load whatever,
to quickly fly away,

before the masses make it back,
make it back across the track.

Yes, back.
They were here before,
before there was a track,
before there was a there,
on the other side of here.
For then there was no other side,
then there was no there,
before we built the track,
down the middle of us all,
and made two sides,
them and us,
before the ducks began to sing,
before the pigs began to prance,
before the docs began to quack,
before the bishops begged for cash,
before the preachers looked away,
before the lawyers and the judges
began to waddle in their fat,
before the teachers taught their lies,
before the merchants overcharged,
before we all began to belch.

THE COUNTRY MUSIC STAR

Please take me down to Ryman Town;
I'll sing some songs while there.
I'll don a glitzy gaudy gown,
and belt my tunes with flair.

But songs I sing in Ryman Town
will never be the same
as those I sing without the gown
in towns I cannot name.

I sing in pubs and grungy bars
in tiny friendly towns,
and dance a jig with all those stars
who sing without the gowns.

The Angel of Thirst

When my thirsty yearning people come to drink from
deeper streams,
to quench the greatest thirst of man,
a thirst beyond their dreams,
they leave the land of shallow springs,
and come to deeper waters here,
and for a time their thirst abates –
for a season, perhaps a year.
But always, always, their thirst returns,
and then again they come,
when their thirsting spirit yearns
to draw from deeper waters here,
to quench the greatest thirst of man,
a thirst beyond their dreams;
they drink, and drink, and drink,
these yearning thirsty people, in the land of deeper streams.

And The Thirsty Say:

We drink deeply, we who thirst,
and yet we never get enough.
Before the coming dreadful drought
we drink our fill,
and then for seasons go without.

But in its time our thirst compels:
we find and sound those ancient wells,
or dip our cups in flowing streams
that give us life beyond our dreams;
and from them draw their crystal healing waters,
and then we drink, and drink, and drink, again,
we who thirst.

THE TRIP TO CAMBRIDGE TOWN

I'm traveling down to Cambridge town
to get to know my inner scribe.
I've not yet worn its scrivener's gown
but think that there my one true tribe
will greet me well with pen and ink,
and urge me on to dream and think.

I'm on my way to Cambridge town
with pen and ink and skin,
and when I've donned my scriveners
gown
I'll beg them let me in.

THE WARRIOR

I am the king, the commander in chief.
He was a general of the army,
a man of the nation,
born of the nation,
protector of the nation,
protector of the people,
and of their land.

I summon the general,
and I tell him to go and kill the enemy.
And he goes,
and he kills,
he goes into their land
and he kills.
And then the enemy sends generals to our land,
and they kill.
They kill us.

I send for the general,
and his generals,
and they come and the general says to me,
"Your Majesty, we kill the enemy
and our enemy kills their enemy,
us,

and we are at war.
We kill them, they kill us,
we are at war."

And so I consider this war
and I ask the generals what it will take to win the war,
and the generals talk to me.

"We must kill many more of the enemy."

"We must destroy his food supply."

"We must make him want to end the war."

"We must degrade his weapons and stockpiles."

"We must have more and better spies than him."

"We must kill more of the enemy. We are not killing
enough."

And one general says to me:

"My colleagues give good counsel.
But,
Your Majesty,
We cannot win this war.

No one can win this war.
Most wars are neither won nor lost;
Most wars are just stopped.
They kill, we kill, and then we all stop killing.
The war stops.
We do not win the war; we end the war.
When I say We,
Your Majesty,
that includes the enemy."

This general had my attention.
I wanted to hear more from him.
"What would you propose that we do to end this war?"
"Commander, Your Majesty,
you begin by heeding the counsel of my fellow generals.
You even heighten our effort,
as we move into this last phase of this war.
But we must know that the enemy will do the same.
As we continue to destroy and kill,
and be destroyed and killed,
by our enemy,
we will send word,
through our back channels,
that we can see,
in the distance,
an end to this war,
that there is no longer a need to kill and destroy.

Your Majesty,
we will tell our enemy,
through our back channels,
that perhaps soon our people can intermingle, and
intermarry,
and trade goods,
and maybe,
maybe,
friendships destroyed by this war can be renewed,
and our descendants can live in peace,
without having to bear the memory of these horrors.
That is the message that you should send to our enemy.
But,
Your Majesty,
there is one principle,
one,
that I would humbly urge the king, Your Majesty, to
consider,
and it is this:
It is easier to be enemies,
than it is to be friends.
The king must count the cost of friendship,
Your Majesty."

And so I listened to this subordinate general,
and I gathered him to my staff to counsel me.

Because of him
I can see an end to this war.

Life On The Mountain

You want me to move down off the mountain?
I like living up on the mountain.
It's quieter up here.
The air is cleaner.
I can see things at greater distances,
and my dogs can run greater distances,
and they can do their business where they will,
without bothering my neighbors,
who live at greater distances from me
than neighbors live from each other in the towns,
down in the valley,
where the dogs cannot do their business where they will,
because the neighbors of the dog owners,
down there off the mountain,
are afraid they will step in the dogs' business.

So some nitwit down there says they will have to pass a city
ordinance,
making it a crime for dogs to do their business.
But the hard fact of the matter is that dogs must do their
business.

So the people down in the towns in the valley,
they have to write the law very carefully,

so that it is clear that the criminal is not the dog,
but rather the dog's owner,
because in every instance the defense of necessity would be
available to the dog,
because dogs absolutely have to do their business.
It's a necessity.
And as everyone on the planet knows,
necessity is a defense in criminal cases.

So this ordinance, this law,
must make the dog owner the criminal,
not because the owner owns a dog or two,
but because the owner allows
the dog to do his business,
while running free,
unleashed,
in somebody else's front yard,
or on the sidewalk,
where passersby might step in it,
and get a good portion of the dog's business
stuck on the bottom of their shoe,
or even on the bottom of their bare foot,
if they are going about barefooted,
which some would surely say
should be a crime in itself,
because that could be very unhealthy.

So these people who have business on the bottom of their shoe,
or even on the bottom of their bare feet,
perhaps squishing up the side a little bit,
and maybe even some who don't,
but who can imagine how awful it would be,
to get dog business on the bottom of their shoe,
or their bare foot,
perhaps squishing up the side a little bit,
in their imagination,
these people pass a law,
making it a misdemeanor for a dog owner to allow his dogs,
or her dogs,
to run free and unleashed,
in the town down off the mountain.

Note that most of these ordinances only require leashing the dogs.
The owner can still carefully guide the dog to a (despised) neighbor's yard,
especially during the potty walk,
just before bedtime,
in the dark,
without violating the ordinance,
as long as the dog remains on a leash.

So here's the scenario that I see sometimes,
or at least I imagine sometimes,
when I go down off the mountain,
to buy things in the towns in the valley,
or at least imagine that I am doing so:
If the dog enforcement officer happens by,
(In almost all instances it would be in a motor vehicle)
when a dog is just beginning to arch,
in preparation for doing his, or her, business on the
sidewalk,
the owner can simply drag the dog into the gutter,
and won't be charged with a crime,
as long as he doesn't kick the dog,
which I would never do,
or otherwise abuse it,
as he is dragging the dog into the gutter,
before he, the dog,
or she, the dog,
does his or her business illegally on the sidewalk,
instead of in the gutter.

And if the owner interrupts the dog sufficiently,
while the dog is in the gutter before doing his or her business
there,
after the dog officer drives by,
the owner can drag the dog back into the (despised)

neighbor's yard,
where the dog can re-arch and do his or her business there.

Frankly I would rather just live up here on the mountain,
with few neighbors,
with unleashed dogs,
and without sidewalks,
or gutters,
if that works for you.
I love you, Baby.

THE BACK OF THE PLANE

"Ladies and gentlemen,
This is your cabin attendant speaking to you today,
from the back of the plane.
We are preparing for our descent,
into chaos and turmoil
and who knows what else in New York.
As many of you know,
right about now we would be instructing you
to fasten your seatbelts
but our captain has told us to inform you
that we have a special treat for you today.
He has assigned one of his trainees
to land the airplane today,
because the guy still needs to get certified,
and based upon our captain's experience as the guy's
instructor,
neither a seat belt nor anything else will help
if this guy doesn't do better than he did
the last time he took this test and landed the plane.
To be fair, no one was killed in that landing,
but just shy of 100 travelers were hospitalized for several
weeks.
I really can't say much more about that at this time,
because of various privacy laws,

that restrict us significantly,
and also of course because of pending litigation.
As always, privacy is front and center
when we are discussing the incompetence of any of our
employees.
In any event we can't do anything about it right now,
because a few minutes ago when the pilot and the real
copilot
stepped out of the cockpit to go to the toilet,
(their toilet in the cockpit is out of order)
the trainee,
who's flying the plane right now,
locked them out of the cockpit.

But not to worry.
The captain says dude has improved his landing skills
and should be able to take her down, this time,
without too much of a bounce,
so the captain has decided to let you choose
whether to lock yourself into one position,
or to sit loosely in your seat,
or even get up and walk around
to give yourself some flexibility during the landing.
Out of an abundance of caution,
and dedication to our customers,
the captain has even asked us to open the liquor cabinets to
all,

during this descent.
Thank you, ladies and gentlemen,
We hope you enjoy your stay in Atlanta.

Wait, here comes the captain now.
It looks like he's raided the liquor cabinet himself,
and is headed back here!
Cool!
He's got his pockets stuffed with these little liquor bottles
from up in first class!
They say the safest place in a crash is back here.
Looks like party time to me!"

NOTE

This selection, *homodeus*, is a bit unusual in that some of the poems in it appear as passages in more than one place in this same publication. This is because *Homo*, which I view as one poem, is made up of many poems, and has been for almost fifty years. At this stage of my life any publication that is offered as a selection of my poetry must certainly include *Homo*. But it also should contain many of these poems in Homo that also stand on their own. In my own soul I sense resonances in the duplication that I like.

However, if the repetition bores you or irritates you, I would offer some counsel given me by my good friend Jehangir Chubb many years ago: If you are bored to the point of exhaustion, take a nap. If you are irritable and it's 2 o'clock in the morning and you can't sleep, get up. Reread whatever it is that's bothering you and eat a couple of boiled eggs. There's nothing like the taste of a boiled egg following an encounter with a masterpiece.

-Joe

Homo

CRISTOLOGO

A train whose name was Yesterday
Came thundering down that track.
You know the one.
That same track on which Tomorrow
thundered in….
From east and west
A hundred thousand tons of steel
Came screaming,
Screaming down that track,
And crashed….
The track is gone,
The steel is gone,
The thing is done.
But if you will come along with me,
I will show you where it happened:
I was there,
Sitting on a bench,
In a little station,
In a village whose name was Now,
Waiting to catch my train.

Come With Me

So come with me, but know that you do not come this way
If not wonderingly, and open, and true;
This seeks discoverously;
This bespeaks, and apprehends and
distributes ambiguously;
(Are you listening?)
This weeps and laughs and hurts.
This points to certain secrets that will
delight you.

HOMODEUS

Prolegomena to Any Future Metaphysics
(With Apologies to Immanuel Kant)

deus

homo

homodeus

deus

PART ONE

Hilda

1

The old man raised his hand and slashed it down hard. It met neck right behind the creature's ears. There was a solid crunch and a brief convulsion.

The old man immediately took a sharp steel blade and cut the creature's head off and then let the carcass hang there and bleed. This must be done before the heart stopped pumping. Then he cut the skin around each hind leg, cut across the crotch, severed the front feet, and peeled the hide down. He drew the guts, then cut the organ meat from them to keep for himself, and tossed the rest to his dogs. He broke the hind legs at the first joint and cut through them there with his blade, and then he tossed the carcass into a wooden box that earlier he had half filled with snow. He filled the box with more snow, covering the creature; the meat would be more easily cut after it chilled. He picked up the box and walked into his cabin.

2

The night had come, and the old man now walked in the
forest. Snow flew about his boots as they ploughed deep,
marking a trail to tell the occasional wanderer whence he
had come.

But the wanderer in this forest, for the moment, was he.
The old house deep therein had been good for him; he
eventually found himself there when he was tired and
needed to ponder. There, in the night, he could be rested.
He raked the snow from a spot on the porch and sat.
He watched – the distant winking windows; the chimney
sparks showering down on moonlit scapes…

High, high fly the yearning spirits;
High fly the seekers;
High fly the comers and the goers,
And the gazers at the comers and the goers,
And the gazers at these;
And the greeters and the talkers –
Ah, the greeters and the talkers –
How high they fly…

At first the old man thought about her.
He pondered the thing,

the blood, and the pain, and the tears,

and those recollections transformed him, and he went
deeper and deeper,

Till anguish tore at his gnawing, boiling innards;

He saw her and the dead baby

And afterwards he saw her dead,

While he waited and wondered,

And watched for the dawn…

I'll spend these deep, dark seasons

Where howling winds blow cold and fierce,

And roaring flames rage hot, and long,

And where searing memories of you, my Love,

Sustain me through the long, long night.

Breathe into me, holy Lord of all,

And be my muse,

That from this come truth alone,

And that when these words

Have failed to exhibit the fullness of

Your immense, immeasurable holiness,

As they shall,

I will somehow bow me further down,

And let you take me home.

Slowly out of the night they came. Slowly, out of the bedded
leaves,

from deep in the caves,

stretching and gazing about they came,

moving away from the dens,

and the night,

and the night mind,

and out onto the pebbly slopes,

leading down below,

where the dew-tender grains of the wild-grass patch awaited

them.

I've looked out across you,

And seen the whole of you,

Homo;

I've seen your comings and your goings,

And I've seen you recline as one across whole lands, as day

turns into night.

And I've seen you rise all with the dawn,

And take up your tools and your weapons,

And set out upon your roads and your trails,

And go into the forests and the fields,

And assert yourself.

And your groupings of habitations have amazed me,

Homo.

Domus!

Civitatem! How can I speak of them?

How can I tell of the application of your paws

To stone and wood,

To iron and earth.

And the mixing of your mortar,
And the shaping of your spikes,
And then with them the making of your hut,
And then the placing of another and another
Till there are many, together;
You congregate, Homo!
I have long sought to view you from a metaspecial
perspective,
And yet I cannot do it;
I cannot do it completely, Homo,
For your utterances make sense to me,
And your motions are my motions:
There have been times when I would have Locked my paw
around a club,
And a stout one, too!
And set out meanly upon the trail
Toward your agglomeration
To injure and to kill:
I know you Homo.

(THE RESOLUTION)

The hunter crouched in the glade, in the tall grass,
And slowly, silently, took one long arrow from his pouch
And nocked it; he must not let this moment pass
Without its long awaited, long sought resolution.
The hunted paused, in the shade, by the tall grass,
And rested, kneeling, full aware that his ablution,
In the temple, had resolved nothing alas,
For the one who would have his soul, who crouched in the
glade.
The hunter aimed his arrow, from the tall grass,
And drew it; and every fiber in him tensed, replayed
The passions of a thousand pains that would never pass,
And then released. Watching, the hunter slowly rose from
his crouch.

And the poet was the one who watched the ones who
watched the ones who gathered grain in the wild-grass patch.

3

I am the storyteller's poet,
Admirer of threads and of
threads of threads,
And willing talker thereabout.
I seek all their connections.
I am that percipient essence before which
there is the ceaseless query.
Perhaps it could even be said of me
that I am the query.
(It is true that from time to time
I succumb to the machinations of man;
But in the end I am true to you,
My Song,
For in the end it is the poet who sings.)

4

The Opposite Shore

From among those beings in the dim past
he had wandered, and had gone on.
Why? He had asked, and had gone on, till
he came to the brink of the deep, and looked.
It is too late, he said.
And the chasm returned with the reply,
Why?
He died! He cried.
Said the chasm, Who?
Me!
You?
Yes, he muttered, and gazed,
From the brink of the deep,
To the opposite shore.
Said the chasm, Where?
There, he said, and pointed from the
brink to the opposite shore.
Then why are you here?
Here?
I don't know, he said, and gazed,
from the brink of the deep,
to the opposite shore.

5

The baby's half dead
And I'm about to freeze.
Put some wood on that fire!
Mama's sick and cain't work no more.
What d'yuh mean there ain't none?
Go chop some.
I'm cold.
I'm sick and tired o' the whole rotten,
stinkin' mess,
You hear me?
These sheets stink.
Seems yuh could at least get some more sheets.
Then wash'em! They stink.
And quit lookin' at me that way.
It's not my fault they busted up m' still.
Ed was gonna fix the leak on the roof
this mornin'
But the damn law took his scooter,
And the shingles were in the saddlebag.
The stupid idiot ought to have carried'em
in his hand dammit,
I don't care if it is cold.
All for two measly pints o' licker,
And I betcha they drank a pint o' licker

And claimed there wont but one pint
I'll guaran damn tee it.
Sam,
Go get them burlap sacks,
And nail'em down on the roof.
Don't you argue with me, boy,
Or I'll kick your teeth in,
You hear me?
Now get up there.
Damn roof.
It's cold as sin
And I can't even keep dry.
Put some WOOD on that fire!
Hilda, I'm goin' to the store.

II
Damn rain.

III
Hey Jim.
Gimme some matches.
Cold, ain't it?
Where's Bud,
After that fancy stuff up the road?
You reckon he'll get it?
I'm gonna tell yuh somethin',
Yuh never can tell.

They say her old man's got money.
I'd like to get my hands on it.
Well, be seein' yuh.

IV
House oughta be warm by now... .

V
Hilda?
HILDA!
You answer me woman, when I call you,
You hear me?
Now shut that baby up.
I'm sick and tired o' hearin' that
fuss ever' minute I'm home.
There ain't no peace o' mind around here.
What d'yuh mean she's hungry?
Feed'er yuh idiot.
What d'yuh mean there ain't no milk?
I bought'er a can day before yesterday!
Shut up,
I ain't got no money.
And quit cryin', will yuh?
Yuh make me nervous....
Hilda, come'ere.
Take this cigar back to the store
And tell'em to give yuh a can o' milk.

I just bought it a little while ago,
And it ain't broke,
So they oughta trade it.
AND SHUT UP THAT CRYIN', WILL YUH!
Take my coat.
And don't you break that cigar,
You hear me woman?
Now go on.
Stupid baby oughta eat fatback,
Like me and the rest.
Ma, you feelin' okay?
Git'er another quilt Liz.
Huh?
Then give'er mine and shut up.
WAIT A MINUTE, don't.
Ma, I'll put my coat over yuh when
Hilda gets back.
It'll dry out.
Put some WOOD on that damn fire!
Damn, that woman better not break my cigar.
Oh Lord, I forgot to tell'er about the HOLE!
That stupid woman,
If that cigar fell out it'll get soaked,
And even if I find it they won't take
it back,
And she won't get no milk,
And the baby'll scream all night!

I"m goin' after Hilda.
Y'all keep that baby warm,
You hear me?

VI

Damn rain.
Maybe she didn't put it in the pocket.
Maybe....
Huh? Is that her comin' yonder? Hilda?
HILDA! Yuh didn't drop my cigar?
It wont broke?
Cold ain't it? Gimme my coat.
Naw, keep the filthy thing.
And shut up that cryin'.
Aw come'ere Hilda.
Don't cry.
We'll be home in a minute.

VII

PUT SOME WOOD ON THAT DAMN FIRE!
It's cold in here, I'm tellin' yuh.
And give that baby some milk.
The roof ain't leakin' no more, Hilda.
I told yuh them burlap sacks'ud do it.
You okay Ma?
Think I'll go to bed....
Come'ere Hilda.

6

My mare I mount, and she gathers.
She gathers and she holds.
(No tears my lady – who can at once
weep and sing?)
She gathers, till we can no more.
She holds, till we can no more.
Princess?
And then together
We fly!

7

We know not why the roles of yesterday
were played,
Nor why tomorrow's greatest dreams
are never lived.
We know not yet why blood was spilled
and children cried,
(All the children God has made
have cried)
Nor why tomorrow blood and tears
will flow again.
But this we know:
Now this we know:
In a little room, in a little house,
we make love today.

Nosotros

I've gone into you, Woman of earth,
Screaming my way into your soul
in that primal moment.
Your rhythms mine, and mine yours,
We've found the path,
And journeyed it together.
In that place where pangs of fear
seize the soul of man,
Where cries of self-sorrow
and the gnawing
and the gnashing
Sound out loudly from this infernal tumult,
I center,
And move on.
Sound the cadence!
Stomp, Stomp,
Here or there a pleasure,
On beyond a woe.
Stomp, Stomp,
On down through the halls of time
We make our way.

One cold day, beneath snow-laden pines,
the old man made his way toward the village.

He had come out of his cabin in the tiny clearing and had
found his path and walked for awhile; now he came out of
the forest and stopped,
and looked toward the village.

He was not too cold;
he had long been a man
in the forest, so it was tolerable.
On this day there was no wind.
There was silence – snow silence.

The old man stood there for a moment and looked, and then
he set out across the fields toward the village.

9

And the old man looked across the fields
and the hills and the forests, and he thought:
Utterly yours I am,
You have given me joy
And bathed me in sorrow;
You have made me see
And left me blind -
And still, I am awed.
Still, I am awed.
ECSTASY!
World within or wherever you may be,
We know you not
For you retreat,
And we know not where.
We know not why, nor how,
But we must assume you have your reasons,
Else you would take our hands,
And walk us through those realms
we call ecstasy.

Do you know that you torture me?
Do you know that you let me stare
And that you cause me to wonder

And that you tantalize me?
And yet you keep your secret.
Do you know that you beckon me,
and then retreat?
A night wanderer you have caused me to be,
A star gazer uncertain,
Till you settle about me
And speak truth to me.
Engage me!
Do not hesitate to trust me with your
cherished knowledge.
Teach me your secrets;
I'll harbor them and use them,
and I'll pass them on to those,
And those only,
Who should have them.

My mane is white.
Today it falls about my shoulders,
flowing.
Tomorrow it may be blowing in the wind.
That I know,
For I have learned.
And then the old man stepped out of the
field and onto the road leading into the village.

10

~ ~ ~

The people who were gathered had asked him to come out of
his little cabin deep in the forest and into the village, for a
great question was to come before them on the morrow.

From among those gathered there in the village that day,
there first arose
three wise men.

And they all said in unison,

The universe is our home.

And then the first wise man said,

Be it ever so humble.

And then the second wise man said,

Be it ever how you wish.

And then the third wise man said,

It is.
And then the three wise men sat down.

11

Then the old man rose and looked at the
people, and the people looked at him.
And a child of the village said to the
old man,
Would you tell us a story?
And the old man was filled with joy, and
he looked at the child, and he loved it. He had been here
many times before, and had told them many stories.
He knew the child within was saying, Where are
you going? Can I go with you?
And the old man said,
Yes, my little friend, I will tell you
the story of a lamb. Listen…listen.

12

The Lamb

In a village in another land, a little boy walked down the street beside a baby elephant. The elephant belonged to the boy's family, and it was the boy's job to feed and water the elephant each day. In that land elephants were very important to the people, for they were used to lift and move things that were too heavy for the people to lift; and when the people of the village had to journey long distances, they rode their elephant if it was their good fortune to have one. The task of caring for a baby elephant was a very important task indeed for a little boy, because the little elephant would grow up someday, and then he would spend the rest of his life helping the people of the village. The little boy was proud that his family had enough faith in him to let him care for their baby elephant.

The sun was shining brightly at this time of day and almost everyone in the village had gone inside his house to escape the heat. The boy walked the little elephant to a water trough which was right at the edge of the village. The elephant began to drink and to spray water over his body with his trunk. The cool water felt good.

The little boy decided to lie down in a shaded spot not far from the trough to get out of the hot sunshine. He lay down on the cool ground and watched his family's baby elephant drink and play in the water.

Lying there on the ground in the shade relaxed the little boy so much that pretty soon it was easier for him to keep his eyes closed than it was to keep them open. Very soon he was sound asleep.

The baby elephant played in the water for awhile and then drank some more, till he had had enough. After awhile he was ready to go back, or do something else.

He walked over to the little boy and gently touched him with the end of his trunk, but the boy was so soundly sleeping that this failed to wake him. The elephant stood there for a few minutes and then touched the boy again, but he kept on sleeping. So the baby elephant decided that he would do something else while his little friend slept.

For some time now, when he would come to drink and play at the water trough, the little elephant had looked at the fields around the village and at the woods beyond the fields. He had often thought it would be nice to walk through the fields and to go into the woods and play for awhile. Today he decided that since he couldn't wake his little friend, he would take that walk that he had been thinking about.

The little elephant ambled through the fields in soft dirt that felt really good to his feet, but what he wanted to do more than anything else was to go into the woods, so he walked on toward them.

Soon the little elephant came to the edge of the woods, and looked in. It was so pretty and cool-looking in there. Everything looked soft and clean and mellow. He decided to walk right on in and explore some.

The woods smelled good. And the baby elephant discovered that when he rubbed against the rough bark of a tree, it felt good. After he had scratched himself for awhile, he walked on, going deeper into the woods. He would see something interesting over this way and he would come have a look at it. Then he would see something else over that way and he would go have a look at that. He rambled all around and did this for a while and really had a lot of fun.

But it wasn't long before he began to get tired. So he decided it was about time to go on back home. The baby elephant started back the way he thought he should, but the more he walked the stranger the trees and bushes looked to him. But he really wanted to go home, so he kept on walking.

Finally the little elephant came to a small clearing and in the middle of it was a pool that was about knee-deep to him. He decided that he would wade into the pool and rest himself there for a few minutes, for by now he was getting really tired of walking and he knew how good the cool water would feel to his feet. He waded in and drank some, and then sprayed his back with water. It felt really good. But after a few more minutes of this, the baby elephant decided it was time to start walking again.

Just as he was getting ready to come out of the pool, he heard a rustling noise a good distance away.

Since elephants are big even when they are babies, the baby elephant couldn't hide behind a tree or bush. He just stood there and looked in the direction of the noise. He could hear it getting closer and closer, but he just kept standing there in the pool in the little clearing, looking. And then, right out of the bushes and right into the clearing trotted a baby lion.

Big lions can hurt baby elephants, but when they are still young, lions and elephants are not afraid of each other. They just think about things like playing together. And that is just what the baby elephant started thinking about. He raised his trunk and made a happy sound through his mouth and started splashing over toward the baby lion to smell him and play some. But the little lion wouldn't pay any attention to him. He just trotted right through the clearing with his nose close to the ground.

The elephant still wanted to play, though, so he ambled along behind the baby lion, trying to get his attention, but the lion just kept on trotting, with his nose close to the ground, and with the little elephant ambling along behind him.

Soon they were deep into the woods again, and they just kept on going. The baby elephant had his attention focused on his little lion friend and completely forgot about trying to find his way home.

Pretty soon the baby lion, with the baby elephant right behind him, came to the edge of the woods and stepped into a field. He didn't even slow down. He just kept his nose to the ground and trotted on and the baby elephant stayed right behind him because he still wanted to play some as soon as the little lion got to wherever he was going.

The baby lion kept trotting and the elephant kept ambling along behind him. And then, all of a sudden, the little elephant looked up and what he saw made him feel good all over. He was home. He was right at the edge of the little village where he lived.

The baby lion stopped and sniffed around for a moment, and then trotted off in another direction, with his nose still close to the ground. He never did pay any attention to the little elephant who wanted to play with him. The elephant watched him go across the field toward some other woods, and pretty soon he disappeared.

The sun was almost down now, and the little elephant wanted to drink some more water and then get back to his family. He walked around the edge of the village till he came to the water trough. There was the little boy, still asleep. The baby elephant drank some water and then walked over to wake the little boy. He touched him with his trunk and the boy jumped up and said, Oh, No! The sun is about to set! We've got to go right home!

That night, at supper, the father said to his family, Tomorrow we hunt the old lion. She came today and took a lamb.

13

The old man looked at the child for a long moment, and said no more. Then he looked long at the people, saying nothing, and then he turned and left the village, and went back across the fields and back onto the trails leading back to the tiny cabin deep within the forest.

And then that night the old man left his cabin and once again found himself a moonlit path.

They ask me what is truth!

Here is truth:

I've gone down the dark road lost,

Then found my way and blissed in light.

And then,

My friends,

I tell you,

In spite of all in me,

I've turned,

And gone back down that dark road lost.

Here is truth:

The rose and the serpent slept together.

The dawn came

And the rose bloomed and spread;

From dewdrops on fragrant petals

Light burst forth,

And we saw life.

Then came the cold,
And into the deepest folds of darkness
The serpent slithered.
Into his abode he drew us,
And it was dark and dismal.
The breath of fear and pain and hate
touched us,
And we saw death.
They ask me what is truth?
They give me the morrow's question
this day?
What is truth?
Here is truth:
That of all that is,
That speaks from every dimension
of every essence,
That singularly undeniable statement,
Made by the rock and made by the bird,
Made by the sun and made by the wind,
And by the stars, and by the tears
and by the pain,
And by the joys and by the hate,
And the sounds and the universes,
And the songs, the screams, the explosions,
and the implosions,
And the crashes,
Here and in all spaces,

And beyond them –
That about all this,
ALL,
That simply says, I am –
That, he thought, is truth.

14

That night clear white light shone in the moonlit forest.
Clear white light that bathed the paths and trails that led to
the fields and roads and villages, and to a tiny cabin in a tiny
clearing.
But that night the paths and the trails to the tiny cabin in the
tiny clearing were no more trod.

They found the old man some time later. In the evening they
laid him out on a slab of stone in the forest.
Soon he was gone.

Gone?

15

When all is done,
When day is gone
And dusk has faded;
And when I know that I have heard my song,
And looked upon it and considered it,
and smiled,
Then, I turn gently toward
the fatherland.
Then I must go my way,
For this is the way the world is.
Likewise, you must go yours.
I cannot be with you when you come upon
your first hurdle,
Nor can I open those doors you closed,
For this is the way the world is.
I cannot comfort you nor can I brush
tears from your cheeks
When you weep for something you know not.
For now, I must be without you,
For this is the way the world is.
We must walk away,
And walk, and walk, and walk,

Till our paths shall converge,

And we shall move hand in hand

Through a world we've come to know.

16

As you go yonder way,
Mark a path there for me.
I'm going that way too,
When I finish here.

Gone, my Love, are the high winds and the soaring eagles.
Grim is the night.
Dim are the night beings and the night mind;
Gone is the light.

PART TWO

Hawkness

1

I come.

I present myself.

I make my statement:

The songs I shall sing to you,

peoples of the universe,

Will be of my essence;

It can be no other way,

And you must know that now.

I accept the call, but I come to you

poet.

The man is gone.

The causes, the theories, the isms,

the differences, the what-ifs,

The great and the small,

yesterday and tomorrow,

Gone.

Just feeling being now,

My joys and my sorrow concurrent

on one blissful hum,

The hum of the harmony of all the

systems of it all,
The hum of God,
The path.
Be it now known to all that
henceforth the doctorates,
the misterates, the madamates,
the sirs, the honorables,
the dishonorables,
Force me no more.
For you I am the poet,
Nothing more, nothing less.
And for me, you are the poet,
nothing more, nothing less.

2

I engage your eyes,
And I see that you know.
And you, you know that I know, and so,
Our brotherhood undeniable,
Peace flows between us and becomes us,
And we are one.
How high we soar!
To you, my love, I lay these presents down.
To you all I have and shall have forever.
Awed I am, and shall be forever.
To you my song I sing.
High, so high we soar!
And I see the nations
of man the animal,
And I see delineations,
And I tell you each and every one
they will fade away.
I come to you with power
incomprehensible,
For I have dreamed,
And I have perceived the family
of sapiens.
We soar…

3

On this day I am the hawk.
I dive,
And all the hawks of all
the ages,
Before and to come,
Rush on this dive.
(For one brief moment,
In the totality of it all,
This form is here,
In the all-being.
It blinks into shape once,
It quivers,
And then it is gone.
Gone.
But something goes on.
It's there in the storyteller's soul,
And in the marble cornerstone
of homo's domicile,
This thing that moves on
through us all,
And does not stop when
each we do,
But moves on,
Becoming more with

each birth,
And yet even more with
each demise,
Transversing generations and
constituting them each,
Expressing them all,
And being expressed by them,
This thing.
So this song issues from it all.
As much yours as mine it is,
and no claim to it shall be held
lest it be in favor of all.)
Imagine!
The whole thing, at once
shuddering, trembling, rumbling,
As earthward we rush on this dive,
Anticipators of the scream of contact,
Of this moment's truth:
The union the Word:
A morsel in our gut,
That all the children of all our children
of all the ages,
May dive.

4

God All.
God the tree.
God the bird. God grass.
God fences and pastures.
God cows, horses, mules, and pigs.
God leaves, water, and stone.
God the highs, God the hassles,
God the smooth sailing.
God the illusions of man,
God you, God me,
God All.

5

Go into the night!
Count every star in the heavens.
Go roam the valleys,
And climb the mountains,
And sail the oceans:
Then come to me and let me gently
whisper in your ear -
I'll say to you, In all time,
You will not see what I have perceived
in one timeless flash.

6

I've stood at the foot of the mountain

and looked up.

I've soared to the peak

and looked down.

I've stood inside

and looked out,

I've stood outside

and looked in.

So come, my friends,

Sail to me on those gentle waters,

And see that I shall

enfold you,

And dwell with you and in you forever,

And shall never, ever leave you.

Now come.

7

But know you this: From my soul will I sing as much as
from my mind.
If thinker you would have me
always be,
You will go wanting,
For poet I am,
I am.

Epilogue

When a poet tenders his work, he in effect invites an audience to participate with him in something that is very central to him. But to conceive of his written work as being this central thing is to commit a mistake that impedes appreciation of that which really is central; the written work is the medium that the poet uses to involve his invited guests, and re-involve himself, in his most essential intercourse with reality – not just in its logic and facts, but in its joys and sorrows and questions, in its mysteries and beauties.

In doing this, however, he does not always say outright what he means for the participant to grasp or experience. He speaks on different levels; and if the participant is moved by the discovery of a connection between elements of the poetry, he may assume that it has probably become apparent to the poet, too. For the poet is continually involved with his work. He, more than anyone, is sensitive to its weaknesses, to its failures to embody in language what he wants to convey, so he returns to it over and over, trying again and again, being presented again and again with what his language is about. And he notices the connections, and indeed may work with his language to proffer a connection more clearly. Moreover, the poet uses his medium to discover, and one who participates with him in the poetry can use it to discover. This is very much what the art is about. So the poet says, Come, listen with me and be amazed with me at what these words reveal and signal and touch deep within. His work is about something, and he, better than anyone, knows this. What he is seeking, when he turns back to the poetic within him again and again, is beyond words in the end, but its spirit dwells in the words and forms which are delivered to him and which he is so compelled to seek. With the coming of these words and forms comes the joy of discovery; and the poet says, Come see, and rejoice with me. In these deeper reaches we will come to know each other. But this is concomitant. It is not the poet's intent to reveal himself in his work; his intent is to reveal something else, but in the process he does uncover himself, if only by indications in his language that he was or is moved to discover this or that and that he has thought about it.

So it is with Homo. I have been very involved with it for many years, and I have paid close attention, I think, to every word in it. It is still growing, and what there already is of it contains much yet for me to discover, I suspect. It is not tendered as a final, completed poem, but rather as a work that continues to develop and grow, but which is nonetheless sufficiently mature to provide me with very great pleasure in sharing it. I hope there will be those who will enjoy it as much as I have, who will live it, in some degree, the way I have.

A philosopher friend of mine told me, "Hardly anyone will know you or listen to you. You won't make much money. Very few people read poetry. It can take many years for you to become known. Poets have a very small audience." I thought, but did not say, some poets have an audience of one. But the roads and the reasons of a poet are not much considered when he hears the call. He does not know how to refuse the call.

On a personal note, I am deeply grateful to Elizabeth O'Berry, a high school teacher who encouraged me in the birth of my poetry when I was in my mid-teens, and to Sam Ragan, Southern publisher and poet, who took time to read some of my early poetry over six decades ago when he was editor of the Raleigh News and Observer, giving me needed encouragement then. I am especially grateful to Claire Miller of the UNC Department of Philosophy, who was remarkably skilled at navigating and skirting bureaucracies if necessary, and Michael Resnik, chairman of the Department of Philosophy who admitted me as a walk-in graduate student, and Maynard Adams, Kenan Professor of Philosophy and formerly Chairman of the Faculty of the University of North Carolina at Chapel Hill. He gave me an office next to his in Caldwell Hall. With some exceptions we met daily for a brief discussion, usually early in the morning. One morning shortly after I had written Story of the Lamb we were in his office and I handed him a copy of it. He read it and looked up, slightly frowning, apparently genuinely puzzled, and asked "So what's the point?" Without hesitation I said "Well, the point is that often things inure to our benefit without our knowing it." He paused for a moment and his expression changed to one of perception and affirmation as he looked straight at me and nodded slowly and said "Sure they do." That moment was special to both of us, and I will never forget it. He was rather animated for a while that day following that discussion. He encouraged me and sustained me and reinforced my belief in Homo; but more importantly, he was one with whom I experienced the deep satisfaction of having a meeting of the minds.

Joe Edwards

Cookeville, Tennessee

www.ingramcontent.com/pod-product-compliance
Lightning Source LLC
Chambersburg PA
CBHW031342060726
47590CB00007B/2589